The Princess and the Pea

Retold by Susanna Davidson

Illustrated by
Mike Gordon

Reading Consultant: Alison Kelly
Roehampton University

Contents

Chapter 1

The picky prince

Once upon a time there was a prince who wanted to marry a princess. But he didn't want just any old princess. He wanted a *real* one.

This is Princess Cordelia, Your Highness.

Not one of the local princesses would do.

"What's the matter with them, Patrick?" cried his father, the king. "I'm running out of princesses to show you."

Are they too old? Too tall? Too hairy?

"I can't be sure they're real," sighed Prince Patrick. "I'll have to find one for myself."

"You must do whatever you want, darling," said the queen, who spoiled him rotten.

The next day Prince Patrick set out to travel the world, in search of a real princess.

He took with him twelve suitcases, ten pairs of shoes, a spare crown and his cousin, Fred.

"Goodbye, my love," cried the queen, wiping away a tear with her silk handkerchief.

They hadn't gone far when
they heard a loud sneeze from
under the seat.

"Who's there?" shouted
the prince.

A small figure crept out.

It's Peg!

"Aren't you the palace
maid?" said Prince Patrick.

Peg nodded.

"Well, what are you doing here?" the prince asked.

"I want to see the world," said Peg. "I've been at the palace all my life – ever since I was left on the doorstep as a baby."

I want an adventure!

She blushed. "And Cook's furious because I burned the pudding," she added.

"Well you can't come with us," said Fred. "This is a boys-only adventure."

"We're not turning back now," said Prince Patrick. "She'll have to join us."

10

Peg grinned at Fred.

"OK," Prince Patrick went on. "First stop, the wicked witch's hut."

Fred looked alarmed. "You are joking?"

Prince Patrick shook his head. "The witch will know how to find a real princess. She's my best hope..."

Chapter 2

Off to see the witch

"Now Peg," said Prince Patrick, "this could be dangerous. You stay in the coach. Fred and I will meet the witch."

The prince knocked three times on the witch's door... There was no answer.

Why couldn't I stay in the coach?

"Looks like no one's in. We'll have to go," said Fred, who was already backing away.

13

"She must be in," said the prince, and he bent down to peer through the keyhole.

A large green eye was staring at him. Prince Patrick jumped back and landed bottom-first in a patch of mud.

A short plump woman opened the door, chuckling to herself. "Did I scare you? I was just checking who you were. You can't be too careful these days."

Look at this mud!

Fred was amazed. "Are you the witch?" he asked. "You're not scary at all."

The witch looked rather upset. "I try my best," she sighed. "I grew three new warts last week."

"Come inside," she added. "I'm just cooking some tasty soup for lunch."

"We're not hungry," said Prince Patrick quickly. "I've come to ask for your help. I want to know how to find a real princess."

"Real princesses are very rare," said the witch, "and it's hard to spot a fake one. But there is a test you can do."

Let me see...

"A real princess must have... boiled brains, rotten beans and cat spit."

"What?" cried the prince.

"Oh sorry, that's a recipe for soup. This is it..."

The real princess test

A real princess must possess ...

1. Politeness to one and all

2. Kindness to rich and poor

3. Very sensitive skin

"Sensitive skin?" Prince Patrick asked, looking confused.

"A real princess," explained the witch, "has such tender skin that she could feel a pea under twenty mattresses."

"Thank you," said the prince. "You've been very helpful." He turned to the door.

"Oh do stay for lunch," pleaded the witch. "My soup's almost ready."

No... really.

I insist! And bring in that poor girl from outside.

Urgh! I can't eat that!

They were stuck in the witch's hut until the cauldron was empty.

"I feel sick," groaned Peg on the way back to the coach.

"Well, you shouldn't have had three bowls then," said Fred.

I poured mine into a plant pot.

"I was being polite! I didn't want to hurt the witch's feelings."

"That was very kind of you, Peg," said Prince Patrick, smiling at her.

"Where are we going now?" asked Fred.

"Now I have the witch's test, I can finally find a real princess," said the prince. "We're off to meet Princess Prunella. Check the map, Fred."

Princess Map

Princess Prudence

Princess Prunella

Princess Primrose

Princess Pavlova

Chapter 3

Princess Prunella

Princess Prunella was very excited to see the prince.

"You must come and stay in my castle," she cried.

She raced over the bridge, dragging Prince Patrick with her. "Hurry! Hurry!" she called to her servants.

He's perfect.
We'll be married
in no time.

"I want you to prepare the best bedchambers for the prince and Fred."

"Excuse me," said Peg,
struggling with all the luggage.
"Where am I to sleep?"

"Maids belong in the attic,"
replied the princess, haughtily.
"There might be a few mice
there, but I'm sure you'll cope."

Peg went to her room. It was cold and damp. She could hear mice scuttling about, squeaking.

The prince can't marry her...

Meanwhile, Fred and the prince were in the grand dining room with Princess Prunella.

"You're being very kind," said Prince Patrick, "but what about Peg? Is she eating in the kitchen?"

The princess looked shocked. "Your beastly little maid? You can't expect *me* to bother with *her*."

She can eat the pig slops if she's hungry.

"I'm afraid we must leave," said Prince Patrick. "You're not a real princess after all."

26

"Oh yes I am!" cried
Princess Prunella.

"Oh no you're not!" shouted
Fred. "You've failed the first
real princess test."

Rats!

"Real princesses are polite to
everyone," explained Prince
Patrick, "and you've just been
rude to Peg."

Chapter 4

Princess Pavlova

"I won't give up!" said Prince Patrick. "There must be a real princess somewhere..."

"According to this map, there's a Princess Pavlova next door. Let's try her," Fred suggested.

Princess Pavlova greeted them all very politely.

"What a pleasure to have you here," she said. "Welcome to my castle."

Thank you, Your Highness.

"She's passed the politeness test," thought the prince. "Now what's the next one..."

"Fred!" he cried, "I have a plan. I'm going to dress up as a beggar and see if Princess Pavlova is kind to me."

"Try out your disguise on Peg first," said Fred, "to make sure it works."

Prince Patrick found Peg sitting on a tree stump, about to eat an apple.

I'm a hungry beggar. Have you any food for me?

"Oh you poor thing!" Peg cried, when she saw him. "Here, have my apple."

Prince Patrick was very
pleased with himself. "Excellent!
It works," he shouted, throwing
off his disguise.

It's you!

"What are you doing?"
asked Peg. But the prince
was already knocking on the
castle door, to try the test on
Princess Pavlova.

A servant answered.

"Is someone there?" called Princess Pavlova.

"It's a beggar, Your Highness."

"We've got nothing for him," snapped the princess. "Tell him to go away."

And he smells.

Prince Patrick turned away.

"She's not a real princess," he thought. "A real princess is both polite *and* kind – even to beggars."

Chapter 5

A real princess

I'll never be married.

"I give up," said the prince, with a sigh. "I don't think there's a real princess anywhere. We may as well go home."

They got ready for the long journey back to the palace. Everyone was glum, even the horses.

I bet Cook hasn't forgotten about the pudding I burned.

The coach arrived at the palace just in time. A huge storm was brewing.

Peg was sent straight to the kitchens in disgrace. "You've got hundreds of dishes to wash," scolded the cook. "They've been piling up since you left."

Prince Patrick and Fred went to find the king and queen. Outside, rain began beating against the windows. Streaks of lightning lit up the sky.

Just then, there was a knock
on the door.

"There is a Princess Primrose
to see you, Your Highness,"
said the footman.

Not another one!

A beautiful princess stepped
into the room. She was wet from
the rain and shaking with cold.

"I'm so sorry to trouble
you," she said politely,
"but my coach has
broken down."

"No trouble at all," said Prince Patrick quickly. "Why don't you stay the night at our castle? We'll fix your coach in the morning."

Thank you! I must give you something in return.

"She acts like a real princess," thought the prince, "but I must be sure."

3. Very sensitive skin

He asked the servants to prepare Princess Primrose's bedroom.

"I want twenty mattresses on the bed," ordered Prince Patrick, "and a pea at the very bottom."

Here's your bed, Your Highness.

It's rather high...

Peg didn't get to bed that night. She had to finish washing the dishes.

The next morning, Princess Primrose came down for breakfast, looking refreshed.

"How did you sleep?" asked Prince Patrick.

I slept like a baby.

"I loved all those mattresses," the princess said. "It was the most comfortable bed."

40

Prince Patrick sighed. "A real princess would have felt that pea," he thought. He waved goodbye to Princess Primrose as soon as breakfast was over.

Another fake one!

She's not good enough for my Patrick.

It was Peg's job to clean the princess's bedroom. Slowly, she climbed up the ladder, yawning with each step.

"I'll just lie down for a moment," Peg thought, "before I start cleaning up."

Zzzzzzz

In no time at all, she was fast asleep.

An hour later, Peg woke with a start.

"Ow!" she said. "There's something really lumpy in this bed. I'm getting down."

Ooh. It's a long way.

But as she leaned over, she knocked the ladder. It clattered to the ground.

"Drat!" Peg cried. "I'm stuck."

"Help!" she shouted, as loudly as she could, "I'm stuck. Please... HELP!"

Everyone rushed into the bedroom.

"What are you doing up there?" Prince Patrick called.

"I was supposed to be cleaning," said Peg, "but I was so tired I fell asleep."

"And there's something horribly hard in this bed," she added. "I'm covered in bruises."

This can only mean one thing.

"I can't believe it!" cried the prince. "You were polite to the witch, kind to a beggar and now you've felt a pea under twenty mattresses. *You* must be a real princess!"

He raced up the ladder. "Peg, will you marry me?"

Peg gasped. "You want to marry *me*, a palace maid? Yes please!"

A maid?

But a princess at heart!

"Three cheers for Princess Peg," shouted Fred, and everyone cheered.

So Prince Patrick finally married his real princess. He put the pea in a glass case in the palace museum for everyone to see.

It may still be there today...

The Princess and the Pea was first told by Hans Christian Andersen. He was born in Denmark in 1805, the son of a poor shoemaker. He left home at fourteen to seek his fortune and became famous all over the world as a writer of fairy tales.

Series editor: Lesley Sims

Designed by Russell Punter and Natacha Goransky

Digital illustration by Carl Gordon

First published in 2004 by Usborne Publishing Ltd., Usborne House, 83-85 Saffron Hill, London EC1N 8RT, England. www.usborne.com
Copyright © 2004 Usborne Publishing Ltd.